Behind the Mask

Shai Lenore

This is for all the people who are tired of being walked all over and treated like they're nothing. You can't do what Cindy did, but maybe reading about it will make you feel better.

Contents

Author's Note

Please be aware that although this is a Cinderella retelling, it includes mature themes and is intended for readers 18+. Some things you can find in Behind the Mask include:

Death

Blood

Murder

Child abuse

Drugs/drugging

Addiction/enabling an addict

Sexual assault (off page)

Erotophonophilia

Your mental health matters.

ONE
Three Weeks Before

CINDY

Standing in the isle of the thrift store, I glare at Grace.

"What's your problem?" she asks as if she doesn't know.

"I don't understand why you want to go to this stupid party," I reply with a scowl. "Besides, it's not even Halloween!"

Grace turns to me with her eyebrow raised. "What the hell does Halloween have to do with anything?"

"It's a party with *masks*, Grace. You wear masks at Halloween." I roll my eyes, annoyed.

"It's a *masquerade*, you doorknob!" Grace sighs at my questioning look. "Like, a ball. You dress up and wear fancy masks. We're not talking Ghostface or Michael Myers here. We're talking pretty, lacy masks with long, flowing dresses and stuff."

"You mean to tell me that a bunch of frat-house boys are planning some sort of masked ball?" I roll my eyes at her again. "Jay's one of the ones in charge of planning this. You know that, don't you?"

"Yes, Cindy. I heard you the first fifty times you said it." Grace moves down the rack, digging through the dresses but not seeming to actually *look* at any of them. "And if you guys were still dating, you'd be first in line to go. Don't even try to tell me you wouldn't," she says just before I can protest. "It's insulting that you'd think I'm that dumb."

I don't say anything for a couple seconds. There's no denying that Grace is right. "But don't you see why I *wouldn't* want to go now?"

Grace stops her perusal to glower at me. "It's not his fault what happened to you at that party, Cindy! And I don't blame him for not wanting to stay with you.

"Elliot invited me and told me to bring you. He said we'd have fun. Besides, everyone will be wearing masks, and you won't even have to be around Jay if you don't want to. I don't see what the big deal is! It's not like it's some small party. They literally rented out a whole place for it and everything."

Sighing, I relent. I've long since given up trying to convince Grace of the wrongness of what happened that night. She's decided to be willfully ignorant about it.

Grace has liked Elliot for as long as I can remember, and now he's finally single, so she's doing whatever she can to spend time with him, hoping they can get to know each other better.

When Jay and I started dating in grade eleven, she was so excited because we could all hang out as a group sometimes. But then Elliot got a girlfriend, and she was always there when we hung out.

Jay and I dated for two years before I realised we both wanted different things. I should have just ended it, I know that, but I guess I was comfortable and didn't want to deal with the change. So I stayed even though it wasn't what I wanted anymore.

I keep digging through the dresses, waiting for Grace to start talking again. I know she's annoyed with me for being a major asshole, and I don't blame her. She's always willing to do the things I want without much complaint; I should do the same for her.

After a couple minutes of quiet searching, she pulls out an emerald-coloured gown. It's long and sleek, some sort of silky material.

"You could wear this, then you'll look like it's Christmas time with that bright red hair of yours," she says sarcastically, holding it up to the ends of my hair. "Why'd you have to go and dye it that colour?"

Grabbing it, I frown. "I thought it looked good!"

"Yeah, when Mrs. Claus runs out of red thread to fix Santa's suit, she'll just call you and see if she can steal a couple strands of your hair."

"Rude!" I laugh. She's just teasing, but now I'm starting to wonder if it really does look bad.

"Okay, fine. It doesn't look *that* bad. Just don't run down the street yelling or anything. People might think there's a fire truck coming."

"Grace!" I don't want to laugh, but the way she says it with a completely straight face kills me.

She winks and bumps her hip against mine. "It seriously looks really good. I just can't believe you were actually brave enough to do it!"

"I almost chickened out like four times," I tell her, going back to digging through the dresses. "Remind me again what exactly I'm supposed to be looking for…"

Grace sighs. "I don't know. Maybe we should just go raid my mom's closet. She has lots of fancy dresses from all those fancy events she's always going to." Linking her arm through mine, she drags me from the store.

★★★

Three hours later, Grace's mom has helped us both pick out dresses for the party from her closet. Now we just have to find masks to go with them and figure out what shoes we're going to wear.

The dress Grace is wearing is floor-length red silk, with a deep V-neckline and a slit up one side to about mid-thigh. It looks great with her black hair, but I know she only picked it because her boobs practically fall right out of it. She picked it for Elliot, I'm sure.

I'm wearing a sequined deep purple dress with off-the-shoulder, long sleeves and a sweetheart neckline. It hugs my body to just above my waist and sweeps down to the floor. I don't love to wear dresses, but this one is so beautiful that I don't think I'll mind having to wear it. It's only one night, after all.

"You girls look beautiful in those dresses!" Her mom beams at us. "It'd be wrong of me to make you give them back. Keep them. I have far more than I need anyway."

"Thanks, Mom!"

"Thank you, Mrs. C."

"It's no problem at all!" she says. "Are you girls going to need a ride to the party?"

"No, Mom." Grace rolls her eyes. "I told you; we're just going to take a cab or something, there and back. We're in college now. We don't need our mommies driving us places. How embarrassing!"

Mrs. C chuckles and leaves the room shaking her head, with the rest of her dresses draped over her arm.

"You don't have to be so rude to her, Grace. She was just trying to be nice and make sure we're safe."

"Cindy, you worry about her too much. She can handle it. I was only being honest. Would you want your mother to drive you to a party like that?" She's looking at her phone, probably texting Elliot.

"Sure. If my mother were here to drive me places, I'd let her take me any-freaking-where she wanted to."

Grace's head shoots up. "Oh my God. Cindy, I'm so sorry. I didn't mean it like that. You *know* I didn't mean it like that!"

I sigh because she's right. These days, everyone thinks my step-monster is my mother. I got so tired of correcting people that I just let them believe it. You correct someone, then they want to know where your mom is. That means you have to tell them she died, and then you get those awful, pity-filled stares.

Sure, I'm sad that my mom is gone. I'll probably always be sad about all the things she's going to miss in my life—and the things she already *has* missed. But I'm grateful that she's not in pain anymore. It's a complicated thing.

"Well, the good news is that we have dresses now!" Grace always changes the subject when things get awkward. It makes me wonder if anything ever fazes her. "And I found us some masks online! I ordered them."

When I go to ask her how much I owe her, she puts her hand up and rolls her eyes. This is something that happens regularly, when she buys me a coffee, or we go out for lunch. I'll never get used to it.

"Okay, well, if I don't get home soon, Linda's going to lose her shit. I didn't do any chores today, and she set me up with a giant list before she went to the spa."

"I don't know why you don't just tell that bitch off or tell your dad that she treats you like you're a slave or something."

"I know you don't, but I'm not going to do either of those things—which is something that I know *you* know. I'll text you later," I tell her as I make my way out of her room.

Two
One Hour After

CINDY

I shiver as I sit at the small table in the interrogation room. I'm not sure how long I've been sitting here waiting, but it feels like forever. It makes me wonder if they didn't put a clock in here on purpose.

When I got here, I stumbled in looking something like the girl in that old movie where they dump pig blood on her. One of the officers was kind enough to get me something to wear and some cloths to wipe myself off with, but I really just want to get home so I can shower.

The door opens and two cops come in, one carrying a sweater that looks like it'll probably be way too big on me, and the other has a bottle of water. I can't imagine why they think I'll need these things when they could just send me home.

"Hey there, Cindy," the one with the sweater says. "My name is Detective Delgado. This is my partner, Detective White. We understand you've had a pretty rough night, but we're going to have to ask you some questions."

"What do you mean? I already talked to that other officer… Can't I just go home?"

"I'm afraid not. I need to get as much information from you as I can, so we can find out who did this." She gives me a sympathetic look. "I know it's not going to be easy, so you can take your time. But it really is important that you tell me what you know now, while it's still fresh in your mind."

Sighing, I nod. I get what she's saying, but I really just want to go home, shower, then go to bed—I'm exhausted from the events of the last couple of days.

"All right. But don't you have to call my parents first?"

The detectives share a look before the one who called herself Delgado says, "Well, since you're legally an adult, we actually don't have to do that. But if you'd like for them to be here, we can get a hold of them."

"Yes, please. That would be great… I'm glad that my dad is in town for once." My eyes start to widen as the words fall out of my mouth and I put my head down, closing my eyes.

"Detective White will go make the phone call, but you and I are going to start here while he does that, okay?"

"Sure," I tell her, even though I want to say no way. I don't want to talk about it, not to her. Her silent partner leaves the room to call my parents.

"All right, let's start at the beginning. Tell me everything you know about the party and the people who threw it."

"Honestly, not much… My friend Grace was the one who decided we were going. When that girl made a decision there was no changing her mind. So we got her mom to let us use a couple of her dresses, and then Grace bought the masks online somewhere…

"I tried to find her before I left, but I didn't see anyone else, and I didn't want to start touching the… the…

"Oh, God." I start to cry. I don't want to do this part. What can I possibly say to them?

"Calm down," the detective says, passing me the box of tissues that was on the table. I take one and wipe my eyes with it. "Take your time and try not to worry too much about anything else. There are detectives on the scene right now, and if your friend is there, they will find her."

"Okay." I nod and try to think of what to tell her next. "She got invited by the guy she was talking to, Elliot. He and a couple of other frat boys were planning the party. Honestly, I was surprised when she told me about it, 'cause why would frat boys want to have a masquerade?

"But she really wanted to go because she wanted to impress him, so I just let her drag me along."

"You're doing great, Cindy. Now I want you to tell me about what happened when you got there." She's smiling slightly, probably to encourage me to continue.

"Well, when we got there, we had to sign in. Then we had to put all of our belongings into little baggies, that we wrote our names on, and toss them in a big lockbox.

"I didn't know ahead of time, but it was actually supposed to be a lock-in, a device-free lock-in. When I found that out, I wanted to go home. But Grace had already paid for us to get in and the guys at the door were being dicks about there being 'no refunds'…"

I take a breath, trying to think of what to say next. The detective slides the water bottle across the table to me, and I open it to take a sip.

"I tried to relax and just have some fun, and for a while, I did… but at some point, Grace was gone, and I tried to look for her, but I couldn't find her anywhere. So I just stayed along the sides, hoping to catch her if she went to get a drink or use the bathroom. I never ended up seeing her."

Detective White slips back into the room, leans down, and says something into Detective Delgado's ear. She nods as he straightens and crosses his arms over his chest. I take a deep breath before continuing.

"When they told us about the lock-in at the door, they also told us about the rooms they made up for the night… We'd be staying in rooms with a bunch of other people…

"Anyway, I decided to just go hang out in there because I couldn't find Grace and I didn't want to stand around by myself anymore. I didn't know if I knew any of the other people there because of the masks, and I didn't really want to try to find out."

I'm distracted when Detective White moves to a chair in the corner and sits, arms still folded, watching me.

I clear my throat, eyes flicking back to Detective Delgado. "Anyway… I left the room at one point to go to the bathroom. When I went in, I slipped in a bit of b-blood." A sob tears from my chest. I take a breath, appearing to steady myself before I continue.

"I didn't think anything of the blood because I've been to a *lot* of parties and seen some pretty nasty things… People are seriously disgusting when they're drinking or doing drugs… or both. I just figured some nasty jerk left a mess behind after having… lady problems.

"After that, I was really not going back to the party because I was covered in someone else's bodily fluids, and I didn't have anything to change into. So I went straight back to the room.

"When I next decided to venture out a couple of hours later, hoping to find Grace and convince her to come to bed… it was *awful*." I work to make it look like I'm trying to hold in the sob this time, then I let it out. I blink my eyes a few times before new tears begin rolling down my cheeks. "It was a bloodbath out there," I tell them between sobs. "I never saw so much blood in my whole life!"

Just then an officer pokes their head in the door, and Detective White stands from his seat in the corner to make his way over. He steps out with the officer, and I try to compose myself while he's gone.

I'm blowing my nose when he re-enters the room. Just like last time, he leans over to say something to Detective Delgado, while also passing her a paper. He then returns to his seat in the corner, eyes glued on me.

"Cindy, I'm going to stop you there for a minute, okay?" Detective Delgado regards me, almost curiously. Then she turns her attention to the paper in her hands.

"Sure." I sniffle.

"When Detective White tried to get into contact with your parents, there was no answer on the phone."

"Did you try their cell phones? I gave that officer their numbers when I first got here."

"I know you did." She nudges the box of tissues a little closer. "Detective White tried both cell phone numbers and the house number. There was no answer on any of them, so he sent a couple of officers over to your house."

"Thank you. How long until you think they'll be here?" I ask her.

"That's the thing, Cindy... When the officers arrived, the cars were in the driveway, but nobody came to the door when they knocked. So one of the officers tried looking through the windows." She pauses to take a deep breath. "He saw what he believed to be a puddle of blood on the floor, so they entered the house."

I gasp, hands flying to my mouth.

"When they got inside, it was a mess. There was blood all over the place. They went through the whole house and in the end, they found four bodies. I'm sorry to tell you that your parents and your sisters were murdered."

"No, that can't be right. No way…" I want to ask if she's joking, if she thinks this is a great idea for a practical joke. Is that what someone in my shoes would do?

"I'm very sorry, Cindy. Is there someone we can call for you?" Her voice is kind, but that pisses me off.

"No, there is no one else," I tell her before turning my head to stare at the wall beside me.

THREE
Two Days Before

CINDY

"Cindy!" Linda screams from downstairs.

"Coming!" I holler back, rolling my eyes.

I don't really want to go, but I know that if I don't, the consequences will be awful.

My father married Linda three years after my mom died. I was thirteen, the same age as her twin daughters. He thought it was going to be so great. I'd have a mother *and* two sisters. He couldn't have been more wrong.

They started dating and were married six months later. Now, I may not know much about these kinds of things, but I'm pretty sure that six months isn't long enough to really get to know a person all that well.

I tried to tell him this, but he wouldn't listen. He told me that it would be great and that me and my new sisters were going to be "the best of friends." He was wrong about that too.

Linda and her daughters, Chloe and Sally, are literally the devil's spawn. They treat everyone, except my dad apparently, like absolute shit. Since my dad travels a lot for work, he's rarely home to witness any of it. And when he is home, they're all on their best behaviour, so it looks like *I'm* the problem. But the second he leaves, they go back to treating me like shit.

Shortly after they got married, Linda came up with a chores list for each of the kids. It's actually a pretty fair chart, to look at it. The reality is that it's really Cindy's Chores List. When my dad is gone, I'm expected to do *all* the chores on the lists—while her daughters relax and take all of my allowance. When my dad's home, she makes her daughters do the chores assigned to them on the list, to keep up appearances.

When I arrive in the kitchen, where Linda is waiting, I groan. I was hoping my dad would be with her, so she can't be rude to me, but he seems to have found something to occupy his time.

"In two days, your father is taking me, my sister, and her husband out for dinner. You're going to watch their baby while we're gone," she tells me without even looking up from the magazine she's perusing.

"Yeah, not going to happen," I tell her.

Her head shoots up and she glares at me. "Excuse me?"

"You've known for three weeks now that I have a party to go to," I tell her while trying not to rip out my hair. "And I've told you before, I'm not a babysitter. I never even babysat to make money in high school. I don't *like* kids, babies, whatever. I don't like them. I don't want to spend time with them. I'm not babysitting. Tell your sister to stop being cheap and hire someone to watch her drool bucket."

"Whoa, whoa, whoa," Dad says, coming into the kitchen behind me. "What's going on here?"

"Your wife," I tell him through gritted teeth, "is trying to make me babysit her sister's stinking baby when you guys go out for dinner."

Dad chuckles, turning to Linda. "Really? Don't you know Cindy at all? She hates little kids… she hated little kids when she *was* a little kid." He chuckles again. "I don't think you want to do that to the poor baby. Why can't Chloe or Sally babysit?"

"I… Well… I…" She clears her throat. "They've both got plans. They're going to be out with their friends. I figured Cindy could help out her family for one night."

"Normally, I'd agree with you," Dad tells her. "But even I know that Cindy has been planning to go to that masquerade party with Grace that night. We'll come up with another plan for the baby. I'll hire someone if it comes to that." He winks at me and shoos me away.

"In the meantime, you should ask Chloe and Sally again if one of them could watch Nora's baby for a couple of hours," I hear him saying as I make my way back to my room, a smug smile on my face.

Soon, Linda's going to get what's coming to her. She's an evil bitch and I can't wait to see what karma does to her for it. The way she treats people is enough for some horrible punishment, but the way she lets her daughters treat people might be what makes it worse for her.

Aside from helping her to force me to do their chores, her rotten daughters have taken to stealing my clothes, makeup, bags, anything of mine that they like enough to want for themselves.

Not to mention the fact that they've taken to calling me Cinderella, like the princess from that movie. They like to spill things and make messes just to shout, "Cindereeeeeella!"

I've tried ignoring it, since that's not my name, but Linda won't let that fly, so I've resorted to meandering along the halls as slowly as I can when they call for me that way.

One time, Chloe tried to tell me that if they called for Cinderella, they expected a *maid* to show up as she shoved a maid costume at me. Linda shut that one down, but not without laughing about it first.

I hate them, and most days, I hate my dad for bringing them into my life. But I rest easily knowing there's a special place in hell for idiots like them.

Four
One Hour After

CINDY

I sit for a few minutes, silently staring at the wall and thinking about how my life has changed. I have no aunts, uncles, or grandparents to turn to. I am utterly alone. I try to allow the sadness of that thought to wash over me before turning back to Detective Delgado.

"Is there any possibility that the crimes could be connected?" I ask her.

She gives me a puzzled look, then shrugs her shoulders. "I'm not really sure. I suppose it could be possible... But I don't know how likely that is, to be perfectly honest."

"Why not?" I ask her, my temper starting to get the best of me. I take a deep breath. "Am I the only one who thinks this is all too weird to be a coincidence? My family was murdered in our home, while I was at a party where everyone was killed!"

"I will admit, it is very strange. But I don't see how someone could do both things in one night, or why the two incidents would be connected," she tells me.

"Well, shouldn't you be trying to figure it out then?" I shout.

"Cindy, I'm going to have to ask you to calm down. We're going to do everything we can to get all of this figured out." Her voice is so calm, it makes my blood boil. "This means that I'm going to have to ask you even more questions now. Questions about your family. Some of them might be... difficult to answer."

"Fine," I snap. "Whatever you have to do, Detective. I just want this to get figured out so I can get out of here."

"Well, that's great because I want to get all the information I can from you so that I can let you go... well, probably not home, but we'll figure that out when we get there.

"Now, let's start with your father. What does he do for a living?"

"Really?" I say, eyebrow raised. "You're going to tell me that you don't know who my dad was?"

"For argument's sake, let's say that I don't."

"Okay... My dad was the owner of a very successful tech company. They make computers, TVs, cell phones, all kinds of different electronics. He travelled a lot for work because the stuff they make is made and sold around the world, so he had lots of meetings in lots of different places to make sure plants were running properly, and whatever other business-y stuff he had to take care of to keep things running."

"Very good, thank you. Now, do you think it could be possible that during his trips your father has taken a… travelling companion?" At my puzzled look, she continues, "A mistress, if you will?"

"Oh," I say, eyes widening. "I mean, I guess it's *possible*. But if you're asking if I think he would have done something like that? No, I don't."

I didn't notice either of the detectives pull out their notepads, but they're both writing things down as I talk.

"All right, now, do you know if your dad had any problems with anyone? Someone who might hold a grudge against him or something of that nature?"

I take a couple seconds to think about this before shaking my head. "No way, everyone loved my dad. He had a way with people that just made him super likable. I don't think anyone even hated him for having more money than they did…"

"Excellent." She's quiet until she finishes writing on her pad. She looks up at me and says, "Now let's move on to your mother."

"*Step*mother," I correct.

"Some tension in that relationship, then?" she asks, once again writing on her little pad.

"Oh no, of course not. I loved Linda like she was my own mother. It's just that she *wasn't* my mom, you know?" I'm a little sheepish with this answer. "I've always been worried about disrespecting my mom and whatever memories I have of her by 'replacing' her"—I do air quotes when I say this—"with Linda. It was something Linda and I talked about often, actually. Linda always knew how much I loved her, but she respected the relationship I had with my mom enough not to push anything I wasn't comfortable with."

This is turning out to be a lot easier than I had initially thought it would be. It almost makes me giddy. I have to keep reminding myself that I'm supposed to be sad and that I can't let any of my excitement or exhilaration show while I'm here.

"Well, that's great. It sounds like a very healthy relationship." She offers me a small smile.

"It was," I tell her, nodding. I hate lying for Linda, but sometimes we have to do things we don't want to do, for our own benefit.

"What did Linda do for a living?"

"Oh, Linda was a stay-at-home mom. After all, someone had to take care of us girls."

"I see," Detective Delgado mutters as her pen shoots across the paper. "And do you think that given the amount of time your father was away from home, it might be possible that Linda took a lover?"

I giggle and whip my hand up to cover my mouth. "Sorry, it's not funny, not really… It's just that Linda and my dad were so in love with each other, it's almost comical that you'd ask such questions about them. Despite the wonderful relationship I had with Linda, if I even suspected her of cheating on my dad, it would have completely broken that down."

"I get that. I grew up with a stepmom too." She smiles at me again. "And how about any 'enemies' for Linda? Was there anyone she didn't get along with, or maybe you heard her complaining about someone often, anything like that?"

"No, I don't think so. It's like with my dad. Most people loved Linda. I mean, she could be a little hard to handle at first, but once you got to know her, you couldn't help but love her."

The words come easily, even though they feel like acid in my throat. I try to keep my face as neutral as possible.

The detective nods a couple times. "Now, how about those sisters of yours? You guys are the same age, right? You must've been pretty close."

"I mean, I guess so," I hesitate. "I mean, yeah, we were the same age, but we had different interests, different friend groups, that sort of thing. So we didn't really spend much time together outside of family events. But we definitely borrowed each other's clothes and things like that."

"Sounds like pretty typical sister stuff."

"I guess so."

"What did you say their names were, again?"

"Oh, uh, Chloe and Sally. They were twins."

"Right… Did Chloe or Sally have boyfriends?"

"Not that I know of, but like I said… we weren't super close, so I wouldn't be surprised to know that one or both of them had a boyfriend and I just didn't know." I shrug.

"And how did other people like them?"

Another shrug. "I'm not really sure. Like I said, we had different friend groups and stuff. But they had lots of friends. I can't imagine someone who is unlikeable having that many friends."

She finishes writing, then snaps the notepad closed. "All right, we're going to take a break for a bit. Can I bring you anything?"

"Uh, no. I think I'm all right. Do you happen to know when I'll be able to go?"

"Not right now. We have a lot of stuff to get figured out and it's easier if we just keep you here in case we need to ask any more questions."

"Oh, okay," I say quietly, seething as the detectives leave the room.

The Day Before

CINDY

The phone buzzes from the drawer in my desk, and I quietly make my way over to pull it out.

A text message.

> All taken care of. Be there in 10.

Excellent. I move silently around my room, putting on the outfit I chose for this and strapping the homemade knife belt around my waist, then carefully add the knives. Then I pick the burner phone back up and reply.

> Ready whenever you are.

I sit on the edge of my bed, phone in hand, to wait for the text message that tells me it's time to begin. Part of me feels really bad for what I'm about to do, but there's a larger part of me that doesn't feel anything at all.

I waited long enough for karma to do its damn job. I'm *sick* of waiting. So tonight, I'm playing the part of karma. And I can't wait to get started.

The last few months have been filled with planning, changing plans, manipulating other people into making plans or changing plans. I'm exhausted, but I can't give up now, when I'm so close to the end. I have to see it through.

Excitement flows through me as the phone in my hand vibrates again, signalling a text message.

> Outside the door, text me the OK.

A big, wide grin spreads across my face as I quickly type out the agreed upon text.

> Karma's gonna get you for that.

I hurry, as quietly as possible, across the room to put the phone back in the drawer on my desk, then make my way out of the room.

My family thinks I left hours ago, but really, I've been sitting up here preparing for what's to come. I can hear them in the dining room, forks scraping plates and murmured conversations as they eat their dinner. I creep to the top of the stairs, pulling out my personal phone to open the app we use to engage the locks throughout the house.

Elliot slips in the front door and silently closes it behind him. He grins up at me and I give him the thumbs-up once I'm done with the locks. When I reach the bottom of the stairs, I go on my tiptoes to give him a kiss. I step back, nod once, and we separate, going different ways into the dining room, just as we'd planned.

The route I take has me cutting through the kitchen. I'm ecstatic when I enter the room to find Linda. It's so fitting that she should be the first one, since she's the one who ruined my life in the first place. When she notices me in the doorway, she jumps.

"I thought you left!"

I say nothing as I grin and move toward her, my hand wrapping around one of the knives I'm carrying as I carefully slide it out. Her eyes widen when she notices it in my hand, but I'm on her before she can make a sound.

Bringing the knife up in front of her, I slice it across her throat, and blood sprays out over my face and chest. But that's not enough for me. She needs to suffer for all the shit she's put me through.

Grabbing her arm as she starts to fall, I slam her onto the floor before climbing on top of her and stabbing her anywhere and everywhere I can. Face, chest, arms. The knife smashes into the floor once or twice when I miss the latter.

She stopped moving soon after I started stabbing, but that didn't stop me from continuing. My arms begin to grow sore, causing me to stop. I have to get into the dining room to help with the others.

Standing, I roll my shoulders and make my way through the kitchen into the dining room to find that Elliot has tied my dad and stepsisters to their chairs and is holding his gun toward them.

"Aw"—he pouts—"you started the fun without me!"

"Sorry, baby. It was just too good an opportunity to pass up."

I approach him, and he wraps his free hand around my waist, leaning to kiss me. Chloe and Sally are sobbing behind gags Elliot put in their mouths. His ability to get this done has somewhat surprised me. I'm glad I chose him to help me with this.

"You look great in red," he says with a wink.

"Of course I do!"

"So who's first? Well, second, I guess." He chuckles.

"Probably one of Linda's brats. You choose." I smile up at him. "Then I'll get the other one while you take care of dear old Dad." I shoot my father a glare as I say this.

He starts trying to talk through his gag, and I silently instruct Elliot to remove it so I can hear what he has to say.

"What the *hell* is going on, Cindy?" he shouts.

"Really, Daddy? You don't know?" I spit the words at him, letting all my anger come to the surface so he can see just how pissed I am. "I guess I'm not really surprised. You haven't listened to anything I've told you in the last six years, so I guess it makes sense, doesn't it?"

"What are you talking about?" He's frantic now, tugging at the ropes, trying to get out of them.

"You mean you don't remember any of the times I tried to tell you how horrible Linda and her goddamn daughters were to me?"

I start to laugh, then I can't stop, and it starts sounding like the laugh of a maniac. Which, I suppose, is fitting considering the current situation.

"I told you countless times about how Linda forced me to do all the chores while you're away. Mine, Chloe's, and Sally's, while they didn't have to do anything at all. Or how she let them split my allowance and leave me with nothing… I'd tell you to ask your precious wife, but it's a little late for that." I chuckle a little.

"Oh! How about the fact that they decided I was the housemaid? Did you hear about that one? I'm pretty sure that once they realised their mother was just going to make me clean up whatever messes happened around the house, these two"—I point aggressively in their direction with the bloodied knife I'm still holding—"decided to make messes on purpose, just so I'd have to clean them. Then, when that started to get boring, they added a new little touch—they started to call out for 'Cinderella' whenever they needed something cleaned.

"The best part? I wasn't even allowed to ignore it. I had to respond to it, even though it's not my name. And the reference wasn't lost on me, I promise… Have you ever watched *Cinderella*, Daddy?"

"S-sure, Pumpkin," he stutters. "You used to watch those princess movies all the time when you were a kid."

"Oh yeah, that's right! So that means you *must* remember that Cinderella was a young girl who was essentially a slave to her stepmother and stepsisters while they got to laze around all day?"

"I-I guess so, yeah…"

"Maybe if you'd have believed me, your *daughter*, then we wouldn't be in this situation right now. But here we are! All because you had to believe the lie. The act they put on every time you came home so that you'd think I was just being *mean* because I didn't 'like' them or whatever.

"*I'm* your daughter! Me! You should have listened! You should have *believed me*!"

I'm sobbing now, angry at my show of weakness. I swipe at my face in frustration.

"I'm so sorry, Pumpkin." Daddy's crying now too, but I don't feel bad.

"*Stop* calling me that!" I scream at him.

"You don't have to do this, Cindy. Just untie us, and we'll figure this out together, okay?"

"Do you think I'm *stupid*?" I scream at him. "I *do* have to do this! There is no figuring it out." I turn to Elliot. "Put the fucking gag back in. I don't want to hear another word from him. He can watch while we end what's left of his family."

Elliot does what I tell him and then moves to stand in front of the twins, studying them. I know before he makes his choice who it'll be, but I let him take a minute to decide anyway.

I grin as he moves toward Chloe, excited to watch him end her. I learned just a few minutes ago how thrilling it is to take a life. Now I want to see if watching someone take a life is as thrilling as doing it yourself.

He leans over to whisper something in her ear. Her eyes widen, she screams through the gag, and then I hear liquid hitting the floor as she wets herself. I can't help but laugh loudly at that, my cheeks beginning to hurt from how wide I'm smiling and the amount of laughing I'm doing.

Elliot moves to stand behind her chair and she whips her head from side to side, presumably to try to see what he's doing behind her. She's too goddamn stupid to realise that the only way she'd be able to see him back there is if she were an owl. The image in my head makes me laugh again. Who knew this could be so much *fun*?

When Chloe stills, tips her head up, and screams again, excitement floods my body. I can't see what Elliot is doing from this angle, so I move to the left until I can see the side of the chair. He pulls a knife from her back, moves it slightly, and slams it back in through the slats in the chair. He does this a few times before moving back to the front of the chair where he shoves the knife into her stomach and twists it brutally.

He steps back to admire his work, and we both watch in silence as she stops moving and falls still, leaning slightly to the right—toward her sister.

I'm a little disappointed that Sally isn't having much of a reaction to her dead sister's head being almost on her shoulder. But when I look over at her, I see her staring pointedly ahead and realise she's dissociating or something. Now, that won't do at all.

I move to stand in front of her and smack her across the face. She blinks slowly before her eyes focus on me, and I watch the panic set in. When she turns to look at her sister, finding her body limp and hanging toward her, she lets out a scream.

"Screaming isn't going to help you, Sally," I tell her. "Nobody can hear you, and nobody would help you if they *could* hear you.

You're worthless scum. The world will be a better place without you in it."

The tears streaming down her face, smearing her makeup, give me a sense of satisfaction I've never felt before. The thought that I have made her feel this way is the best feeling in the world. So I savour it. I want to remember this moment forever.

I crouch a little so that Sally and I are eye to eye. "I hope you regret treating me the way you did. And I hope there's an extra awful place in hell for you, you wicked bitch." Then I stab her in the gut and force the knife to slide to the right before pulling it back out.

This whole time I can hear the muffled sounds of my dad yelling things at me, but I ignore it. I've made up my mind and I'm not going to let him change it. My heart hurts a little at the thought of getting rid of him, but there's no way I can keep him around after all this. He's part of the reason for my suffering, and he has to pay just like the others.

"Finish it, Elliot," I call over my shoulder as I continue to plunge my knife into Sally. I don't pay much attention to where I'm stabbing her. I just keep stabbing and stabbing until Elliot finally comes over to tell me it's done.

I may have wanted my father taken care of with the rest of this problem, but I didn't want to have to do it myself. That's the only reason I got Elliot to help me. The plan was carefully laid out for him so that he knew he was to take care of my dad while I was otherwise distracted so I wouldn't have to watch.

As much hatred as I had toward him for putting me in this situation and not believing me when I tried to tell him about it, he was still my dad and there will always be a part of me that loves him, no matter what.

I stand and head out of the room without looking at my now dead father. Elliot follows, grabs me by the hips, and pulls me back into him. "That was so much fun, babe. I can't wait for tomorrow night! It's going to be epic!"

I cringe a little when his slobbery lips touch my neck. But as he makes his way to my lips, I find myself more than willing to allow it. I can tell he's used the drugs I gave him yesterday—his habit is getting worse, but I have to keep feeding it so that he'll help me.

Our tongues tangle and Elliot moans, grinding his hips against my ass. Well, shit, I hadn't planned on fucking the slimy bastard, but I kind of *want* to now. The thought makes me shudder—after everything, this might not be such a good idea. But then he's shoving my pants down and his hand is between my legs. I whimper into his mouth.

It isn't until he runs his fingers through my wetness that I realise how turned on I am. Because of him? No, I don't think so... The thought of stabbing Linda to death floods my mind and I almost put a stop to the whole thing—almost.

He breaks the kiss just before he thrusts his fingers inside me. I'm moaning when he whispers, "You look so fucking hot all covered in blood."

I didn't think I would *ever* be horny enough to willingly sleep with Elliot, but I'm learning all kinds of things about myself tonight. I move against his hand as he grabs my breast, pinching my nipple and causing me to cry out.

When he pulls his hand away, I groan in frustration, only for him to spin me around. He throws all the shit off Linda's stupid little decorative table and drops me onto it, lips pressing to mine once again.

He fumbles with his pants, and I hear the sound of the zipper going down, then his cock is pressing at my entrance. Moaning, I shift myself forward, locking my arms around his neck just as he grips my hips and slams me onto him.

The whole time he's pounding into me, my tongue plays with his. But all I can think about is the bloody mess I made of Linda and her daughters with his help.

I'm still thinking of the way the knife felt as I plunged it into their flesh when the orgasm rocks through me. I break the kiss, moaning in ecstasy. Elliot finishes soon after, slamming me down onto his cock one last time as he stills.

Looking down at his blood-covered hands where they hold my hips, I sigh. This was stupid. I can't let anything like this happen tomorrow. It could ruin everything.

He backs away, pulling his pants back up. "I could stay if you want."

I'm shaking my head before he finishes talking. "No. That wasn't part of the plan. *This*"—I gesture between us—"wasn't part of the plan. We have to stick to it from now on."

"If you say so." He rolls his eyes.

"I *do* say so, and since this is my *revenge*, you'll do whatever the fuck I tell you. Now go home, get cleaned up, and go to bed. We need to be ready and well rested for tomorrow." I huff, moving down the hallway to find some sort of cleaner for the table—I don't want to leave any evidence of what just happened.

He's still standing there when I come back, and he watches silently as I clean the table. When I go to move back down the hall, he grabs my arm. My eyes shoot to his. "I'm sorry, okay? I'm going… I'll see you tomorrow."

He doesn't wait for me to respond before turning and heading to the door. I watch him walk away, waiting for him to open the door and step outside before I return the cleaner to its place.

When I'm sure he's gone, I re-engage the locks and head upstairs to shower and get ready for bed just like normal. When I climb into bed, exhausted from the events of the evening, I have a huge smile on my face. It doesn't take me long to fall asleep.

Six
Two Hours After

CINDY

I sit at the table, studying my fingers and wondering what the detectives are up to. I feel like they should have let me leave by now, but I'm not exactly familiar with these kinds of things beyond movies and TV shows.

My eyes shoot to the mirrored glass built into the wall that I know is actually a two-way. They're probably standing there watching me. Do they know what I've done? Have they figured it out?

No way. I was pretty damn convincing, if I do say so myself. There's no way they didn't believe the story I told them. I studied for this. I learned what to say and what not to say. How to behave… This is solid. Nobody is going to figure any of this out. I'm far too smart for that.

Sighing, I fold my arms on the table and rest my head on them, facing the glass, and close my eyes. I'm not going to fall asleep, but maybe I'll let them think I did. I need all the time I can get to think, so I'm going to hope that if they believe I fell asleep, then they'll leave me alone for a while.

The biggest problem I have right now is that I'm not an expert on how these kinds of things work. I have no clue what time it is now, and if I don't hurry and get out of here, my getaway plans are going to be ruined.

I mean, I did the research, but I had to be careful about it, so it didn't leave much room for figuring out all the things I needed to. Now I'm starting to think that maybe I should have risked it.

Or had a completely different plan altogether. I'm starting to mentally kick myself, which is causing panic, which absolutely cannot happen. There can be no panic. I have to stay "cool as a cucumber," as they say.

I need to remember to appear sad and frightened, which I think I'm doing a perfectly good job of—after all, I spent weeks practising in front of the mirror for this.

If only there were some way that I could know what was happening outside this room. What are the investigation teams doing? What have they found? What are those detectives, Delgado and White, doing? Are they just standing on the other side of that glass watching me, or are they trying to poke holes in the story I gave them?

I can't help but wonder how this would have gone if I had never come to the police station for help in the first place. I clearly screwed up on that part of the plan, but it's far too late to go back on it now. All there's left to do is to figure out where to go from here and how to act so that I can get the hell out of here and get out of dodge—for good.

Seven
Twelve Hours Before

Cindy

When I wake up, the first thing I do is check my phone. I find a text from Grace waiting to be read, so I open it up.

> Hay grl! So xcitd 4 2nite!

> Wat time r u gonna b here?

I roll my eyes, annoyed at the way she texts. I've tried to tell her time and time again that it makes her look stupid, but I guess that's fine with her. I type out my answer, telling her I need about an hour to get my stuff together and then I'll head out, before rolling out of bed and going to the bathroom.

The house is peacefully quiet, and I can't help but to pause and soak it all in. I don't feel sad, not even a little bit. I consider the fact that I now have no living parents, and I still remain completely unbothered by it. The only thing I feel is a sense of relief and an even greater feeling that is urging me on to finish the plan and be done with this shithole town and every motherfucker in it.

Grace said she was excited for tonight, but I can almost guarantee that she's nowhere near as excited as I am. Now I have the task of pretending to drag my feet in hopes she changes her mind, which I know absolutely will not happen.

It's an effort to rein in my excited energy, but once I do, it's easier to keep it tamped down.

I head into my closet for my bag and fill it with a couple changes of clothes, my makeup, toiletries, my laptop and its charger, as well as the charger for my phone, and the envelope packed with money and my new ID. I don't want to take anything else that will remind me of this life when I leave because I won't be returning.

I decide to pick up breakfast—I guess it would be more like brunch since it's basically the afternoon now—on my way to Grace's house so that I don't have to work around Linda's body in the kitchen.

So I stop in at my favourite coffee shop and order a large coffee with two cream and three sugar, a couple of pastries, and a sandwich. As I wait for my order, I think about how this is going to be my last time coming here. It's probably the only thing I'm going to miss about this place.

Refusing to let myself dwell on it, I remind myself that there are great coffee shops all over the place and that I'll be able to find one no matter where I go. It's then that I make it my mission to find one *everywhere* I go. Maybe I'll start a travel blog. I heard somewhere that the really successful ones don't even need to have jobs because they get paid to post on whatever platform they use to document their travels. I'll have to look into it some more.

When my order is ready, I grab it and shove a ten-dollar bill into the tip jar, smiling widely at the worker before I turn to leave. Tonight is going to be a *blast*; I just have to get through the torture of getting ready for a party that I wouldn't want to go to on a regular day.

I walk slowly toward Grace's house, munching on my sandwich and coming up with scenarios for tonight. I know I can't predict how anything will actually go when the time comes, but that doesn't take the fun away from imagining it anyway.

Everything better go according to plan, or I'm going to lose my shit. If Elliot didn't make sure that everything was set up the way it was supposed to be, he'll be the first one I take down. Although, he did follow the plan to a T last night, like a little puppy trying to please its master. If he wasn't so infuriatingly disgusting, I might think it was cute. But he's another one who will get what's coming to him, just as soon as his usefulness runs out.

By the time I make it to Grace's house, I've finished my sandwich and both of my pastries. I sip my coffee as I make my way up the walk to the house and ring the doorbell.

I can practically hear Grace squealing as she rushes to answer the door. She throws it wide, screaming, "You're here!"

Giggling, I give her a one-armed hug before following her into the house and up the stairs to her room.

I drop my bag on the floor beside the door and flop down onto her bed with a sigh. The door clicks as she closes it, then she jumps onto the bed beside me.

"That bad?" she asks.

"What?"

"I don't know. That sigh sounded like a 'something-happened-and-now-I-have-to-let-out-some-air' kind of sigh."

"Is that even a thing?" I'm staring at the ceiling, afraid of what will happen if I look at her too much before tonight.

"Duhh! So are you going to tell me what it was about?"

I groan, throwing my arm across my eyes. "Linda was giving me a hard time before I left. Her demon spawn didn't want to watch her sister's sex trophy and she was still trying to tell me that *I* had to." The sister in question got a text message telling her the family caught a bad stomach bug and dinner would have to be rescheduled, as per my plan.

"Ew! She's such a bitch! I seriously don't know why you don't try to set up cameras or something so you can catch her being cunty to you and then show it to your dad."

"That's actually not a bad idea," I tell her. A little frustrated that I hadn't even thought to do something like that. Oh well, too late for that now. "Maybe I'll go out tomorrow or the day after and see if I can find some."

"Hell yeah! We're gonna take the bitch *down*!"

I feel a slight pang in my chest. Although I'm not really sure why. I guess it's probably because Grace and I have been friends since kindergarten. From the moment we met, we've been basically inseparable. She helped me through losing my mom, and she never once left my side. Her mom even let her miss some school so that she could come over and I wouldn't have to be alone.

Not wanting to think about that too much, I push the thoughts from my mind. She's not as good of a friend as she pretends to be. She had me fooled for a long time, but my eyes are *wide* open now.

We might be friends, but she doesn't have my back the way I have hers. If she had come to me with a similar story to the one I came to her with six months ago, I'd have kicked some ass just to get her justice. What did she do? She continuously asked me if I was sure and repeatedly expressed her disbelief at the whole situation.

"Elliot won't show me what he's wearing, or his mask, so you're going to have to help me find him tonight!"

"Fine," I tell her. "Just as long as he's not with Jay."

"There are going to be so many people there, I doubt he'll be anywhere near Jay. And even if he is, you can just stay away from him. Pretend he's not there or something. It's really not that hard, Cindy."

"I know, I know. You're right. What time do you want to start getting ready? 'Cause you have to do my makeup; you know I'm not good with the eye shadow and whatever other powdery shit has to go on."

Grace laughs. "I know. I have it all planned out. But you're going to do my hair, right?"

"Of course, don't I always?"

"You sure do." I glance up just in time to see her wink at me before she gets up and makes her way to her closet, pulling out our dresses. "My mom had these cleaned after we picked them out, so they're all good to go. And the masks are in the box on my desk, but we can leave them there until we're ready to leave."

"Great, sounds like a plan. Now, hair first or makeup?"

"Makeup! I'll do yours and then while I'm doing mine, you can do your hair. After that, you'll do my hair, obviously." She grins at me.

I return her smile. "All right then, let's get started!"

Eight
Two and a Half Hours After

Detective Delgado

I sit at my desk, going over the notes I took and thinking about the young lady in interview room four. Something just isn't adding up to me, but I can't figure out what it is. I know that Paul will probably have a better idea about it than I do—he usually does—but something has me wanting to figure it out myself.

I make a note to ask for the information from the officer she spoke to when she got here—but in writing. It just makes it easier if I can go over the information as often as I want. Plus, I like having it all written out in front of me. Sometimes Paul and I will even lay it all out on a table and try to find any holes or inconsistencies in the statements we receive.

Glancing in the direction of Paul's desk, I see him talking to Cierra, the officer in charge of radio communications tonight. I silently pray that his wife hasn't gone into labour, even though she's not due for another five weeks, because I just know I'm going to need his help with this one.

Paul says something to Cierra. She answers, then he nods and they part ways—her back in the direction of her desk, and him coming toward mine. He sits in the chair beside my desk and sighs. I raise my eyebrow at him and ask, "What was that about?"

"One of the detectives at the scene of that party radioed in."

"Okay… And?"

"And they found one alive. He's not in the best shape, but they're going to bring him to the hospital and hope that someone can get to talk to him soon so we can find out what he knows about what happened tonight."

"Oh, wow. Only the one, though?"

He nods, solemn. "Seems that way, Ri."

"For fuck's sake. Do we know how many bodies?"

"Not yet… There is something else, though."

"Oh?" It comes out sounding like a question, and I suppose it is.

"They found a security room. Like, a hidden room with tons of screens showing cameras all around the place."

"Wow, that's crazy… Let me guess, they were all off or not recording?"

"We're not sure yet, but they have someone on the way to check it out. They're hoping to let us know within the hour, but it could be longer depending on how sophisticated the system is."

I don't say anything, returning my attention to my notepad and flipping the page.

"What's bothering you, Rita?"

I almost chuckle. Paul and I have been partners for five years and he's become the closest friend I have in that time.

"I don't know… Something about that girl doesn't make sense to me," I tell him, brow furrowed as I try to think.

"There's a lot about that girl that doesn't make sense."

I snap my head up to look at him. "What do you mean?"

He shrugs, reaching for his own notepad. He flips through until he gets to the right page and drops it on the desk in front of me. His writing is sloppy, but after five years, I'm pretty good at reading it.

Crocodile tears
Lying about stepmom (stepsisters?)
Sometimes seems too sad, then not very sad at all
Why so eager to leave?
Story seems rehearsed
Emotions don't reach eyes

"Wow."

"Yeah," he says. "Also, something I didn't write down—honestly, it just occurred to me—why did she ask about the crimes being connected? Why would that even be a thought in her head? Nobody told her how her family died."

"I mean, I've never been in a situation where I've just run from a crazy killer, only to learn that my family was also killed… Maybe it's a reasonable thought to have?"

"Maybe… I doubt it, though."

"I hope we hear about those cameras soon. Although I'm not going to lie, I'm not feeling very optimistic about it. They probably made sure those were turned off because of the things that happen at college parties."

"Yeah, but if they're as hidden as I think, maybe nobody knew they were there except the owners of the property—and if that's the case, they're probably up and running so they can make sure nothing illegal was going on or anything."

"All right, I'll give you that one. I guess now it's just a waiting game. The question is, do we let her stew, or do we go back in there?"

"I think we leave her, but I want to go and watch her a bit, see what she's doing in there."

We stand and make our way to the glass, only to find her sleeping with her arms on the table and her head resting on top.

"Odd time to try to sleep, don't you think?" Paul mutters from beside me. I nod in agreement, not taking my eyes off the girl with the bright red hair.

Nine
Five Hours Before

CINDY

Grace and I stand in the line of people dressed to the nines with their fancy masks, waiting to get into what looks like a creepy, old factory. There's excited chatter all around, even though the line is slow-moving. Grace is practically bouncing, she's so excited. I ignore it.

Eventually, we make it to the front of the line where three frat boys wait to greet us.

"Sign in on the clipboard, grab a baggie, put your name on it, and dump all your shit inside. Once you've sealed it, you can put it in the lockbox. Everyone gets their shit back in the morning when the lock-in ends." His voice is a horrid monotone that grates on my nerves.

I widen my eyes and turn to my friend. "Grace! You didn't tell me this was going to be a fucking lock-in! We can't leave until morning?"

"If I'd told you, you wouldn't have come," she whines, pouting. "Besides, you were just going to stay at my house tonight anyways, remember? We'll just be staying here instead! It'll be fun, come on!"

"Okay, but what's this about giving them all our personal shit?"

"Hey, that's the rules, chick. You don't want to do it, you don't get to come in. Nobody gets special treatment. So either grab a fucking bag and put your shit in it or go the fuck home."

I scowl at the dickhead at the door, and when he doesn't back down, I stomp my way over to the clipboard and sign my name, then move on to the bags. I write my name with a red Sharpie, shove my clutch inside, seal it, and toss it into the giant lockbox, then storm away without waiting for Grace.

When she catches up to me, she grabs my arm to stop me from going any farther. "I'm sorry I didn't tell you about the lock-in, okay?"

I glare at her.

"I didn't know about the other stuff, though, I swear!"

"I thought your little boyfriend was helping to run this thing. He didn't think to give you a heads-up?"

"I guess not, but I'll give him shit for it, I promise!" She sighs. "We came here to have fun tonight, Cindy. Let's just forget about the other stuff. It's going to be great!"

I soften a little. "Fine. But if I have a horrible time, you owe me *big*."

Giggling, she throws her arms around me. "You're the *best*, Cindy!"

She drags me through the room to the refreshments table. I stand to the side as she starts picking at the snacks that are set out.

Glancing around the room, I see a decent amount of people, not too many but enough to make it a party. Most of them are just standing around in their fancy dresses or suits and masks, waiting for the party to start—which I already know won't be until after the doors have been locked, ensuring that nobody can get out.

Man, am I ready for this to begin.

Ten
Two and a Half Hours After

Detective Delgado

Paul and I stand there, watching the girl for a while. She remains unnaturally still, and if I couldn't see the slight rise and fall as she breathes, I might think she was dead.

"Do you think she knows we can tell she's not really asleep?" I ask him without taking my eyes off Cindy.

"I get the impression that she believes she's a lot better actress than she really is," he mutters. "Something about this girl is off. I'm going to have someone look into her some. Maybe she has mental health problems or she was a troubled kid. I don't know… There's gotta be something there."

He turns to find someone to do what he wants, then move my attention back to Cindy just in time to watch a smile fade from her face, her eyes still closed.

"What is going on in that head of yours?" I murmur even though she can't hear me.

I feel awful for her. She just lost her whole family in one night, and maybe even a bunch of her friends. But the more I think about it, the more I realise just how right Paul is.

Her story definitely had aspects that were true, but something about it seemed very rehearsed—even her facial expressions seemed like she spent some time practising in the mirror.

Something dawns on me. I turn and move quickly through the room, bypassing first my desk, then Paul's and heading to find Cierra. She's typing something into her computer, the radios silent for the moment.

"Hey, Cee." I lean up against her desk. "Do you know if anyone figured out the name of the survivor down there at that party?"

"Um, I don't think so." Her eyes flick up to my face, curiosity evident in her expression. "Do you want me to find out?"

"You know, I think I do. It's not a huge rush, but as soon as they can figure it out, I'd like to know, please."

"You got it. I'll let them know in just a minute."

I stand to leave when she speaks again.

"Do you think he's the one who did it?"

"I'm not sure, Cierra. But I think that if it wasn't him, he probably knows who it was. I have a hunch; I just want to see what happens with this before I look at it much more."

She nods and moves to pick up her end of the radio as I make my way to my desk where I start to write down my questions and come up with a plan. Eventually, Paul makes his way over again, sinking back into the chair he occupied earlier.

"What's up?"

"I'm not sure yet. I think we need to figure out who that kid was that made it out of there and hope like hell they're going to be okay because I think we're going to have to go and ask some questions."

"You get someone on that already?"

"Talked to Cee a bit ago."

I run my hand down my face and let out a sigh. These kinds of investigations never get any easier. Nobody wants to tell a parent, a spouse, a child, that their family member has been murdered. And there's always that sense of "we have to catch the person responsible *now*."

"You gonna fill me in at all, or just leave me in the dark?"

"Depends on if you'd prefer to hang around in the dark or not, I guess."

"Not this time, pal."

Odd. Usually, Paul has no problem being left in the dark when I'm trying to work something out. Not that I mind having to tell him. Sometimes having two people working on the same thing gets better results.

"I think that maybe we already have the killer here… pretending to sleep in that interrogation room. And if it isn't her, she knows more than she's telling us."

"That so? What's your plan then?"

I raise an eyebrow at him. "Who says I have a plan?"

"Come on, I know you better than that, Rita."

"All right then. I think we wait for the other officers to find out the name of the survivor, and then we go in there to tell her to good news, gauge her reaction—which I'm sure she's going to try to mask. Then you and I head out to go talk to this person, find out what they know.

"We leave Cindy to stew while being closely watched from this side of the glass. When we get back, maybe we poke the bear a bit.

"But in the meantime, I want someone digging, not just for mental health or asshole kid stuff, but looking into her friends and her home life. I want as much as we can get on her, as fast as we can get it. I want everyone who isn't busy with something else working on it."

"I'll set it up," Paul says, standing and making his way to the giant whiteboard at the front of the room. Several officers watch him head that way and immediately drop whatever they're doing to see what he's about to do.

Paul stops in front of the board, studies it for a moment, and decides that whatever is on it isn't important before picking up the eraser and cleaning the board. He picks up a marker and starts writing, his movements catching the attention of more officers.

Cindy Valhalla
17 years old
D.O.B.: 07-27-2004
Victim? Suspect?
Dig into: friends, family, school, everything

When he's done writing, he turns back to the room and clears his throat loudly. The room goes silent, and everybody's attention is on Paul.

"I'm sure you guys have heard about the horrible crimes that were committed tonight. If, for some reason, you haven't yet, let me fill you in.

"Approximately two and a half hours ago, this young lady"—he points at the board behind him—"arrived here covered in blood, ranting about some lunatic at a party killing everyone who was there.

"Officers were dispatched, and it was quickly made apparent that this young lady was telling the truth.

"When Detective Delgado and I went in to interview her, she began asking for her parents. I left the room to contact them with numbers she provided shortly after her arrival. When nobody picked up, I sent a couple officers to the house where they found a brutal murder scene and four bodies.

"We're waiting on more information about how long they had been there before discovery, but I'm expecting an update on that shortly.

"It's been a long time since there was a crime so horrific here, and so we're going to work extra hard to get this solved and make sure this town is safe from the person, or persons, who did this.

"Now, I want anyone who is able to help out. You guys can coordinate and look into different things, but I want everything on Cindy Valhalla, whatever you can find.

"She got suspended in fourth grade? I wanna know, and I want as much information about it as you can get me. Everyone got it?"

Multiple heads nod, then a handful of officers make their way toward the board with clipboards and pens so they can assign jobs. Paul is making his way back to my desk when he pauses.

"I'm also going to need someone who doesn't mind standing around staring for a while, but that'll be a bit later," he announces into the room before continuing over and flopping back into his chair.

Neither of us says anything as we watch the group of officers at the front coordinating and taking jobs before they break apart and head back to their respective desks.

In the silence, I replay as much of the interview with Cindy as I can, when something occurs to me. "Paul…"

"Hmmm?" He glances over at me, clearly having just been pulled from his own thoughts.

"Do you think, maybe… Well, do you recall the words Cindy used when she was talking about her family in there?"

His brow furrows, and he tilts his head slightly. "Not sure I know what you mean, Ri."

"Well, I was kind of going over our conversation with her… When we told her that her family was murdered, she *seemed* disbelieving, right?"

"Yeah, I guess. So what?"

"Don't you typically find that people who are shocked by the death of a loved one take more than fifteen seconds to start talking about them in past tense? Like, a lot longer? Hours, days even?"

His eyes shoot up from where he was looking at the paperclip he was bending out of shape. "She did start with that pretty fast, didn't she?"

"Someone needs to call the coroner, now. I want to know how long those people were dead for when they were found."

ELEVEN
Six Months Before

CINDY

I pound on the front door of Grace's house relentlessly, hoping someone answers quickly. Then the door is tugged open and I'm staring into the smiling face of Mrs. C, just before her smile falls as she sees the tears pouring down my face.

"Grace is in her room, honey," she tells me, stepping aside to let me through the door. I hurry past her, toward the stairs and Grace's room. "You let me know if you need anything," she calls out from behind me.

When I get to Grace's room, I shove the door open, step inside, and gently close it behind me. At first, I don't think she's in there, finding it hard to see through the tears that refuse to stop. Then I notice her lying on her bed, playing on her phone. I don't think she even looked at me when I came in.

"Grace." I sob.

"What are you doing here, Cindy?" she asks, her voice cold.

"Wh-what do you mean?"

"I heard about what happened last night at that party. Is that why you went on a night that I couldn't go? 'Cause you wanted to be a shitty friend?"

"What are you talking about, Grace?" I nearly shout through my sobs.

She sits up to look at me, hanging her legs over the side of her bed. "I hope you didn't come here thinking your crocodile tears would make me feel bad for you. You know, I never realised you were such a whore, Cindy."

"Why would you say something like that to me?" I'm crying harder now. I'm surprised I even got the words out.

"You have a *boyfriend*," she spits the word at me. "And you *know* that I've had a crush on Elliot for like, *ever*! I don't know what the hell is wrong with you, but it's super shitty of you to do something like that not only to your boyfriend, but also to your *best friend*. And, for the record, I would never do something so shitty to you!"

I take a deep breath, trying to calm myself because clearly Grace has heard something from somebody, and clearly whoever she spoke to is a huge *liar*. When I finally stop sobbing and the tears slow, I look at Grace and see the face of someone I don't even know. She's looking at me with so much contempt that I almost turn around and leave.

"Listen, I don't know who you talked to or what you heard, but I'm pretty sure I was roofied last night and I can't remember *anything*."

"You expect me to believe that story? Ha! I saw the video, Cindy."

I'm so frustrated now. "What fucking video?" I shout at her.

She looks back down at her phone, and I watch as she does some stuff, then turns it toward me. I reach out and take it, watching the video on the screen. My jaw drops and my legs give out, causing me to end up on my ass in the middle of her room. I look up to find her rising from her bed, eyes wide.

"You really don't remember, do you?" Her voice is softer now.

"Who sent this to you?" My voice isn't much more than a whisper.

"Jay. He said he was done with you because you cheated on him last night and when I laughed and told him he was crazy, that you'd never do that to him, he sent me that." She points at her phone, looking sheepish.

"Holy fuck. I think I'm going to be sick," I mutter.

Grace thrusts her garbage pail into my arms just before I begin retching. When I'm done, I find her watching me.

"I'm so sorry, Cindy. I should have known you wouldn't do something like that."

"I can't believe he… And he filmed it? I… Wow…" My breath hitches, and I begin sobbing again.

Grace sits on the floor beside me, takes the pail, and places it on the floor before wrapping her arms around me and pulling me into a hug. I can hear her murmuring things into my hair, but I don't pay much attention to the words coming out of her mouth.

I'm not even crying because I'm sad. I'm crying because I'm fucking pissed. Who the fuck gave Elliot fucking Grant permission to put his greasy, nasty hands on my fucking body? He'll pay for this. And to make matters worse, my best friend, who is supposed to be on *my* side, actually believed that this was something I willingly participated in. What. A. Bitch.

As I sit there, crying from the overwhelming feelings of anger and hatred, a plan starts to form in my mind, and I know I won't rest until I carry it out. A revenge plot, if you will…

Twelve
Three Hours After

Cindy

I remember that day in Grace's room. It's something I think of often. That and the fact that even after watching that video and realising it was involuntary on my part, she *still* continued to try to date that fucking loser. I've used it to help fuel my anger and further my plan. When I had eventually stopped crying, Grace had asked if I wanted to go to the police.

That was laughable. I ended up telling her that it would be better if I didn't because of the people that Elliot hung around with—they'd make my life a living hell if they knew I went to the cops about it. And that was true, but I had already started to come up with a plan to take down all the motherfuckers who wronged me, and going to the police then might've hindered that.

My only regret now is not just making the getaway straight from the party. When I was walking to Grace's that morning, I'd hidden my backpack with my clothes, money, and ID in a predetermined location, so that it would be easy to get when it was time for me to run. I'd just pulled out the bag with my makeup and stuff, flung it over my shoulder, and made my way to her house.

In the months it took me to solidify my plan, I went back and forth on whether I should find someone to help or if I should just work on my own. In the end, I decided I would need someone to help me, whether I wanted it or not. So I went to Elliot.

It was hard, at first, after what he'd done to me. But I just pretended that I wanted him *because* of what he did. I did my best to try to make sure he believed that I liked it and that I thought we were meant to be together. He was more than willing to be with me.

The hard part was when he wanted to take it public, that caused an argument. And then he started acting like an insecure little baby. I had to tell him about my plan at that point. I'd been expecting to have to take drastic measures to prevent him from running off and telling someone, but he was surprisingly quick to agree to go along with it. I'm sure it helped that I was helping him buy his drugs regularly.

Then I told him all about Grace and her pathetic little crush on him. I twisted it a bit, to make him think that I'd always known we "belonged" together, and that she was just trying to get in the way of us.

He loved the idea of toying with her, making her think he was interested and then being there right at the end, so she could see that she'd been played. Besides, as long as he continued to do whatever I wanted, I'd continue to supply him with the drugs he'd gotten hooked on last summer.

He helped me iron out a lot of the details, including the fake ID. But I knew he wouldn't be needing his. And if the police happened to find it in the end, they'd think he was the one who did it and that he was planning on trying to get away afterward. It was a win-win for me.

Except, sitting here now, it doesn't feel like a win at all. I seriously wish I knew what is going on out there. I need to leave before it's too late. I stole enough money from my dad's safe to keep me going for a while, and I figured that I would be gone pretty soon after everything. Evidently, I didn't do enough research on police protocol and how long they keep someone after something like this.

Growing frustrated, I decide to try the door. If it's unlocked, I'm out of here. If it isn't, then I'll just tell them I have to pee or something.

I sit up slowly, stretching and yawning like I've just woken up from a nap. Standing, I stretch some more before making my way to the door and gripping the knob. I start to turn it, but it doesn't go far before it stops moving—locked.

Blowing out a breath, I head back to the table and sit down. I need to come up with a really good plan to get out of here, and quick. The longer those officers spend out there, doing God knows what, the closer they could get to figuring out who did it. And if they do that while I'm still sitting here, that's the end for me.

Reminding myself not to panic, I rack my brain, trying to think of anything that might work. It's going to be hard to come up with a plan when I don't know the layout of this building, but I might be able to make something work anyway.

Thirteen
Karma Time

CINDY

Elliot showed up a little while ago to start dancing with Grace. I knew that as soon as he had her distracted, she'd forget all about me and go on dancing and drinking and doing God knows what kinds of drugs.

There weren't technically supposed to be any drugs on the premises, but you can't exactly stop people from bringing them in in their pockets or whatever. Which is something we'd been counting on.

When Elliot showed me this place, I knew it would be perfect for the plan. Then he told me how there were hidden rooms all over, so we could probably get some weapons and things in before the party and hide them in one. It was probably the smartest thing he'd ever been able to do. And it's going to end up costing him. He just doesn't know it yet.

Every time a new bowl of punch comes out, or a new bottle of alcohol gets opened, one of us finds a way to dose it. He got some stuff from one of his brother's sketchy friends. I'm not exactly sure what it is, but he says it'll put everybody in a decent state for what we need to do. Complete with hallucinations and everything. The hope is that they'll think they're hallucinating the blood and the bodies, and we can get everything done.

I swear, if he's wrong about these drugs and what they're going to do, I'm going to prolong his death and make him wish he weren't such a fuckup. My plan was to spend most of the early part of the night walking around the outskirts of the room, observing and watching for a change in the behaviours of the partygoers. Something that might indicate the drugs have kicked in.

Slowly, over the last few hours, every available drink has been drugged. And since everyone is expecting to be stuck here until morning, everybody is drinking because there's no need for a DD. I've been careful to only drink cups of water from the tap in the bathroom, so my head is clear.

I see Elliot from the corner of my eye. He's groping Grace as she grinds on him. Turning to face them, I see when he notices me. He gives me a thumbs-up, and I make my way out of the room to where we hid the knives. When I come out of the hidden space, I see Elliot leading Grace toward another room, a little farther up the hall, and I trail behind them.

Entering the room, I find Grace on a mattress on the floor. I glance at Elliot, who shoots me a wicked grin as he closes and locks the door behind me. Setting the bag of knives on the floor beside the mattress, I climb on until I'm straddling Grace.

"Cindy?" she asks when she sees it's not Elliot. "When did you get here?" A giggle. "Where did Elliot go? I think we were about to… you know." She winks and then giggles again.

"Elliot's right here, Grace. He didn't leave you. He just misled you a little bit."

"What do you mean?" she asks, frowning. Then her eyes widen. "I *knew* it!"

That puzzles me. "Knew what, Grace?"

"You're totally into Elliot too." More giggles. "God, I can't believe how dumb I am! I should have realised."

I stay silent for a moment, surprised by her words, waiting to see if she continues.

"I'm totally okay with sharing him, sometimes… If we're going to do this, then get started!" Again, she giggles. That shit is getting annoying.

"I think you might be a little confused, Grace." I place my hand on her cheek and watch as her eyes flutter closed. Satisfaction floods my system as I slide my hand down to her neck and squeeze. I reach out with my other hand and Elliot passes me a knife.

Squeezing tighter, I wait for Grace's eyes to pop open before grinning at her and plunging the knife into her chest, once, twice, a third time.

I jump when my dress lifts behind me, my knife held in the air just over Grace's chest as she stares at me wide-eyed—I need to hurry up and finish this.

Just as I begin to turn, I feel Elliot bury his face in my pussy. The shock makes my eyes widen as he starts to eat me out enthusiastically, and when he pinches my thigh, I realise that he expects me to continue. I rock against him slightly before bringing the knife down again. Then over and over, thinking of nothing but the blood coating my hands, until I climax, panting over the body.

When it's over and Elliot stands, coming around to look down at Grace, I sit back a little, looking at her myself. I wait to be hit with sadness at the loss of my best friend, but I feel nothing. Except maybe a giddy need to do it again. And again. And again.

FOURTEEN
Three Hours After

DETECTIVE DELGADO

Paul disappeared a little while ago to find out if there was any word from the coroner about Cindy's family. I've been trying to find stuff about the girl since then. But she didn't seem to ever have gotten herself into trouble before this. Good grades, lots of extracurriculars, no suspensions… By all accounts, this is a perfect child. So what am I missing here? What went wrong with her?

The more I think about the way she was acting while I was questioning her and the way she was answering, the more certain I am that she's somehow involved in all this. The question is, how? And how can I get her to want to tell me about it?

I glance up to see Cierra making her way toward my desk, her tight little curls bouncing behind her in their ponytail. When she reaches my desk, she sits down in the chair Paul normally occupies.

"I heard back about that boy. Name's Elliot Grant. He just turned twenty a couple weeks ago." She hands me a printout with all his information on it. "I printed this out for you 'cause the officer told me they were expecting him to wake up at any moment. So I figured I could just wait and then let you know when he was awake too—which, he is now. Anyway, I gotta get back over there, but I know you guys will figure this out. You and Paul are a power team."

I watch as she walks away, mesmerised by her ringlets. Then Paul steps in the way. "You should just ask her if you can touch them or something."

"What?"

"Her curls. Every time she gets close enough, you stare at them, all amused like a little kid playing with a spring."

"Shut up, Paul." I glower at him. "She got the kid's name and all his info too, apparently. Says he's awake at the hospital, so we might as well make our way there."

"Thought you wanted to go talk to our little friend first."

"Actually, I had another idea while you were on the phone."

"Oh?"

"Yeah. You're going to go in there by yourself," I tell him and his eyebrows shoot up. "You'll go in there, all broody like… And you'll use very few words. I want you to find out which friends of hers were there. Then I want you to drop the bomb about a survivor. Watch her closely because I'm pretty sure it's going to rub her the wrong way."

"Two questions. One: Why am I going in there by myself? And two: Am I supposed to tell her *who* the survivor is?"

"'Cause she sees me as nice. She's going to be more comfortable if I go in there, especially since you haven't said boo to her. And you'll only tell her if she says that Elliot is one of her friends that was there. You know, a 'you'll be relieved to know he's okay' type of deal?"

"All right. I hope you know what you're doing."

"Me too," I tell him as I turn to scan the room. I see one of the rookies at the back of the room filling his coffee cup and bellow, "Darcy!"

He jumps, sloshing coffee all over himself, the table, and the floor before turning to look at me. "Yes, ma'am?"

"You're coming with me," I tell him. "Someone clean up that mess over there!"

I walk away without waiting to see if the rookie follows. Paul chuckles under his breath as I pass by, then heads toward the door to the room, waiting until the rookie comes over by the glass with me before he enters.

I turn to the rookie. "You're going to watch Paul talking to this girl here. Her name is Cindy. Then, when he's done in there, he and I are going to leave. You're going to stand here at this window, watching her and take note of her behaviours while we're gone."

He nods and goes to reply, but I shush him and point toward the glass, turning on the speaker so we can hear.

"Who did you go to the party with?"

"Um, I already told you, my friend Grace."

"Nobody else?"

Cindy shakes her head.

"Maybe you guys met someone there?"

"Well, Grace did. But I was only there 'cause she dragged me there."

"Who?"

"What?"

"You said she met someone there. Who was it?"

"Oh." Cindy hesitates, then, "His name was Elliot. She had a crush on him forever and he recently started showing an interest in her." She shrugs.

"He have a last name?"

"Sure, uh… Grant? I think?"

Paul pretends to look at something on his notepad, nods once, and goes to leave.

"What was that about?" she asks before he can get to the door.

Turning back to look at her, he says, "Well, we got word that there was a survivor. He was taken to the hospital and patched up. His name is Elliot Grant." And with that, Paul leaves the room.

But I'm watching Cindy. Her eyes widen slightly. Then she starts to panic. And I notice when she takes a deep breath to steady herself and school her features.

"Whoa," the rookie says, making me jump. "Did you see that, Detective?"

"I don't know, Darcy, what did *you* see?"

"Her body language changed. When Detective White said that guy's name, she gripped the side of the chair really hard for a couple seconds, then she let it go."

"Did she now?" I ask, amused with the observation.

***

Paul and I head to the hospital a couple blocks away and make our way up to Elliot Grant's room. It's still dark out, a couple hours from dawn, and not many people are out.

When we first get there, his mother is waiting in the hall to give us a hard time for wanting to "bother" her son while he's trying to heal from a traumatic event.

After a few minutes, Elliot yells to her to let us come in and then "go get a coffee or something." She relents, and we enter the room to find the young man lying in the bed with a bandage across his left cheek and one peeking out from the top of the hospital gown he has on.

"Hi there, Elliot. I'm Detective Delgado. This is Detective White. We just have a couple of questions for you. I guess you got lucky tonight."

"Yeah, I guess you could say that. I don't know if it was intentional, or if she was losing her grip on reality or some shit, but she only got me in the shoulder when I'm sure she was hoping for the heart. The knife in the gut didn't go very far or cause much damage.

"I guess it looked a lot worse than it actually was… So you can call it luck if you want. Anyway, you can save the questions 'cause I'm just going to tell you everything you need to know…"

I glance at Paul, then back at Elliot. "What do you mean?"

"I mean, I know what happened tonight, or is it last night now? I don't know. I don't think it matters much." He shrugs. The look on his face is something like sad acceptance. "But I'm going to start by telling you that Cindy Valhalla is a manipulative bitch. And that I might have a bit of a drug problem that she was feeding to get me to help her."

"I'm going to need you to understand that anything you say now can be used against you later," I tell him.

"Oh, I know. I'll likely end up in prison, but that's probably for the best. It's either that or dead on the streets… from the drugs." He sighs and gives us a sad smile.

"I'm going to need you to start from the beginning," I tell him, shocked that this is happening so easily.

"No problem, but you should probably sit down for this."

We move the chairs in the room a little closer to the bed before sitting down. Once we're seated, he begins telling us what happened. Everything I suspected and then some.

Fifteen
Three Hours Ago

Cindy

Grunting and huffing, I stab at the body below me. This was the last one, aside from Elliot. When I'm satisfied, I stand and move away, surveying the room. Most of them were so out of it they didn't realise what was going on, but by the time we were nearing the end, it got a little harder and we had to work together to take them out.

This has been crazier than I thought it would be, but I got to get back at Grace, Jay, and all their friends who were sharing that awful video, plus a couple extras. And now, it's Elliot's turn. This is the one I've really been waiting for. I can't wait to watch the life leave this scumbag's eyes.

After Grace, I told him no more touching until the job was done. He comes over now and kisses me, wrapping his arms around my waist and dragging me from the room, down the hall, back to where Grace's body still lies on the mattress where I ended her life.

Elliot drops down beside her, shoving her off and onto the floor before pulling me on top of him. "Let's do this quick so we can get out of here," he says with a grin, and I almost laugh out loud at the fact that he thinks he's going to leave here alive tonight.

"You do have the keys, though, right?" I ask.

"Right here," he says, tapping his front pocket and making the keys jingle a bit.

"That's great," I tell him with a big smile on my face. I lean down until I'm hovering just over his face and reach out with my right hand to make sure the knife I left behind is still there. I smash my lips to his as I wrap my hand around his cock, pumping it up and down.

Positioning him at my entrance, I sink onto him with a moan. I figure that I might as well get what I can from him, after what he took from me that led us to this moment.

I begin to ride him, thinking only of the people we killed. The way their blood sprayed from them, coating my face, hands, and arms. My dress is ruined, but I'm not overly sad about it. I revel in the memory of the feeling of the knives penetrating skin, even the times I felt it smack into bone.

When my climax is close and Elliot's hands are gripping my hips, I lean forward and wrap my hand around the knife. Bringing it up in the air, I sit up as I plunge it into his chest, chasing my orgasm.

I twist the knife, yelling out as I come. He reaches up to grip my hand like he wants to push it away or something. When he looks at me, his eyes are wide with shock that quickly turns to anger.

"You. Bitch. Why?"

"Because I fucking can. And because you're a sick, junky pig with no place in this world." I laugh as I pull the knife out and slice it across his face before bringing it down and stabbing him in the stomach. "Besides, you're no longer useful to me."

Dropping the knife, I dig my hand into his pocket and pull out the keys. Dangling them in front of his face, I tell him, "I'd say it was nice knowing you, but it *really* wasn't. I hope you enjoy hell. You can say hi to my dad for me."

I stand and make my way to the door, where I use the key and go out into the night, heading toward the police station to report an *awful* crime. I toss the keys into the bushes as I pass, smiling to myself at the job well done.

Sixteen

Five Hours After

DETECTIVE DELGADO

When we got back to the station, we had all the information we needed to cuff Cindy and charge her with multiple murders. Including a written confession from her partner.

The story Elliot told us was an interesting one. But it made complete sense. He was able to get his mom to bring us the phone he used to communicate with her regarding the plan she had come up with and that he helped to fine-tune.

It's always a sad day when we have to arrest such young people, with so much potential. But the fact of the matter is that we can't have dangerous people like them walking around if we can help it, and thankfully in this case, we can.

Elliot's mother was less than impressed when we had to cuff him to his hospital bed and call an officer to stand outside his door until he's able to be released into police custody.

As soon as we walk through the doors, Cierra comes to greet us. "They did what you said, and we have all the footage of the night here now. They're reviewing it, making copies, all that fun stuff. But there was one shot I wanted you to see. I think that if you hadn't just gotten a confession from her partner, this probably would have sold you on Cindy's guilt.

"Oh, and the coroner's office called. They're saying the bodies were there for at least twenty-four hours, possibly longer."

That's a little longer than what I was expecting to hear, but it makes sense. I wonder if she left and stayed somewhere else after, or if she spent the night in that house with the bodies just left where they were. Did she get ready for the party there too? I guess it doesn't really matter very much anymore. We have what we need to arrest her.

Cierra leads us into a room with a screen paused on the outside of the old factory building that those college kids rented for their party. When she presses play on the tape, we all watch as Cindy meanders out of the building, without a care in the world.

She's covered from head to toe in blood and is walking with the carelessness of someone out on their evening stroll, with no impending tasks or demons chasing them. Certainly not like someone who just barely walked out of a blood bath, like she claims.

Cierra presses another button and now we're seeing Cindy at a different angle, more of the front of her than before. I watch as slowly, a big, maniacal grin spreads over her face. When she nears the bushes at the end of the property, she tosses something into them and turns out onto the street to make her way here, where she believed she'd get away with her crimes.

Turning to Cierra, I hand her the paper containing the confession of Elliot Grant. "I'd like three or four copies of this, please."

She takes the paper and turns to leave. "Actually, Cierra, if you wouldn't mind… Could you drop one of those copies on the table in room four, please."

Cierra shakes her head and shoots me a wink before leaving the room to head to the copy machine.

"If you don't ask her out, I'm going to do it on your behalf." Paul nudges me on his way out of the room, chuckling.

"That's not fair!" I call after him, trailing behind him to look in on Cindy and wait for Cierra to bring her a copy of Elliot's confession.

"Hey, Detectives," Darcy is still standing watching Cindy. "I don't really have much to report. She's been pretty jittery, though. Bouncing around, some pacing. Sometimes she was looking a little like she was… constipated." He blushes. "But after a while, I realised that it was just because she was trying to stay still, or a little more still than she was being anyway…"

"Thank you, Darcy. You did an excellent job. Go take a break. You earned it." I watch him walk away before turning to Paul. "I don't get why you care so much."

"Maybe because you're my friend." He bumps me with his hip. "You live for your work, but you deserve to be happy too. Cierra is someone who gets it. And you like her."

I roll my eyes and go back to watching Cindy as she fights to sit still. Darcy wasn't wrong about her looking constipated. It almost makes me giggle. Almost. But this isn't a laughing matter. And most of me is just sad that this young woman has ended up in this situation, that something went so wrong for her somewhere that she decided this was a good route to take.

It's not long before Cierra enters the room, walks briskly to the table, places the sheet of paper in front of Cindy, and leaves just as quickly as she went in. Instead of going back to her desk, she comes to stand beside me and watch as Cindy reads the confession Elliot wrote out.

Her face grows increasingly red the further she gets in her reading. Eventually, she balls up the paper, whips it across the room, and pounds her fists on the table, letting out a shriek that we can hear even without turning the speakers on.

"Well, that's enough of a confession for me," Paul says. "You wanna go cuff her?"

I check my watch. My shift ended fifteen minutes ago. I look at my partner, shake my head, and tell him, "Not this one. I don't like arresting these ones… I'll get the next one. Besides, I've got to get home to Milo. He'll be waiting for his walk and if I make him wait too long, he might just pee on the couch again."

Paul shakes his head, a slight smile on his face as I turn to head home. Usually, it takes much longer to crack a case or get a confession, but I'm glad it went quickly this time around—I'm not sure how long I could have looked at that girl, knowing she wasn't right, without losing my mind.

I collect my stuff from my desk, punch out, then head home to bring my dog for his walk. And hopefully get some shut-eye before I have to come back here and do it all again.

Breaking News!
Mass Murder at Frat Party

Police are investigating after masquerade ball thrown by college fraternity turned bloody.

Investigators say there are two survivors of the grisly event.

19-year-old Cindy Valhalla, daughter of tech company owner Calvin Valhalla, found her way into the police department, covered in blood, in the early hours of the morning.

Initially, investigators believed her to be the sole survivor of the incident, but later a young man was found alive at the scene of the crime. 20-year-old Elliot Grant was rushed to the hospital with serious injuries.

Tech company owner, Calvin Valhalla, and family found dead in their home— possibly in relation to fraternity party massacre.

Police arrived at the Valhalla home after attempts to reach the family, at the request of 19-year-old Cindy Valhalla, went unanswered. What they found there shocked them.

Detective Rita Delgado of the homicide unit says that officers found four bodies in the home early this morning. 46-year-old Calvin Valhalla, 43-year-old Linda Valhalla, 19-year-old Sally Simmons, and 19-year-old Chloe Simmons were found murdered in their home.

When questioned about the possibility of the murders being related to the massacre at the frat party last night, investigators refused to comment.

Was this a targeted attack, or a home invasion gone wrong?

With Cindy Valhalla linked to both crimes, one can only wonder if this was an attempt to take her life or if there is something more sinister at play here.

Follow along as we bring updates on the story as they become available.

My name is Elliot Grant and this is my confession.

the last two nights, I helped to murder a bunch of people. I wish I could say that it was a stupid decision I made, but that's not the truth. It was months of planning and organising that got us to that point.

When Cindy Valhalla came to me 6 months ago and told me that she wanted me, I wasn't about to say no. It just made it better that she was able to help me score some pills when I needed them. And that's how she got me.

Then she told me that she needed my help with something and I said yes before I even knew what it was. Then I spent months helping her plan.

Two nights ago, we killed her step mom, dad, and step sisters. Then we went our separate ways to get ready for the following night which was when the massacre would really begin.

Even though the party was put together by my frat house, she helped with it a lot. She told me what to tell them to help our plan, and I did whatever she said.

At first, I wasn't sure if she was going to be able to follow through with everything.
Even after we offed her family, I didn't think she's be able to hurt Grace.
but then she did. She went through with everything just the way she said. I don't know why none of it freaked me out then, but it does now.
After she killed her best friend, I should have known she wasn't going to let anyone live. I was stupid enough to think that being on her "team" meant I was safe. But she just used me to finish what she started then tried to do to me what we'd done to the rest of them.
I don't know how many people were there, but we stabbed them all to death. She wanted to make sure they were dead. "No survivors" she said.
There was blood everywhere by the time we were done. Now I can't close my eyes without seeing blood and death.
She stabbed me and left me to die. And I would have if she just did what we were planning and ran for it after she left.
now I'm a murderer and I'm going to hell, but she's coming with me.

Acknowledgements

To my husband, Ryan, thank you for being my rock and supporting me through all of this. I don't know if I'd be able to do this without you. I love you more thank you know.

To my boys, Braydin, Jacoby, and Cooper, just for being awesome and giving me a reason to keep going. I'll continue to chase this dream in hopes that you see it and choose to chase yours too. I love you.

Thank you to Tirzah, who sent me the form to sign up for the anthology this story was originally in, encouraging me to sign up. To Amber for helping her convince me to do it, and to both of you for being a huge part of the reason I decided to write stories to publish. I don't know if I'd be writing for readers at all if it wasn't for you two.

To my Salient Books crew, Jasmine, Monica, Janelle, Georgia, and Tori, thank you for listening to me whine about things, helping walk me through the confusing stuff, and being some of the best friends ever. And an extra big thank you to Jas—for the cover, and because you do way more for me than I ever expected, I hope you know how much I appreciate you. You're all stuck with me forever now, sorry.

Also by Shai Lenore

About the Author

Shai is a Canadian author from Ontario. She grew up getting lost in books and the worlds within them. Eventually her passion for reading turned into a love of creating stories of her own, although they mostly lived in her head until 2023 when she was encouraged to write them.

These days, when she's not spending time with her husband and their three children, you can find her writing dark spicy romance, among other things. Her debut novel, A Twist of Fate, came out in May 2024 and she's been writing as much as she can ever since!

Turn the page for a sneak peek at the first chapter of
***A Twist of Fate*!**

6'0"
5'6"
5'0"
4'6"
4'0"
3'6"
3'0"
2'6"
6'0"
5'6"
5'0"
4'6"
4'0"
3'6"
3'0"
2'6"
BTMPD
CINDY
VALHALLA
MASS MURDER

Frankie

S hoving the last of my things into my bag, I look around the bedroom, sure I'm forgetting something. When I don't see anything of mine, I head to the bathroom to make sure I grabbed everything in there.

Finally satisfied that I haven't left anything in these rooms, I grab my bag and quickly go through the rest of the apartment, looking for anything that might have been missed earlier.

Pulling out my phone and checking the time, I make my way to the front door. I'm cutting it close, but if I hurry, I can be gone before he gets back.

Giving the kitchen one last cursory glance, I place my key on the counter and head through. The front door opens and my heart drops. I freeze.

"Frankie?" he calls out as he comes through the door. "Are you here? I thought I saw your car outside."

I don't answer, hoping he'll somehow not notice me even though I know that's not possible as he rounds the corner into the kitchen, stopping when he spots me.

"Oh, good. I'm glad you came back. Now we can talk about this."

Rage makes my blood boil. He moves closer but stops when I take a step back.

"Don't you want to talk about this, baby?"

"Talk about this? You want to talk about this?" I scream. "Okay, Jack, let's talk about how you were screwing my *best friend* while I was at work! Then we can talk about how I had to walk into the apartment we share and *see* it!"

I know I should probably stop there and just leave—I almost do, but a sick part of me wants to know. "How long? How long have you been sleeping with her in *our* bed?"

My chest is heaving, and I'm sure my face is red, but I don't care if I sound like a psycho screaming at him. He deserves it after betraying my trust like this.

He stands there staring, his mouth opening and closing like he wants to say something, but at this point what's there to say? There's no denying something I saw with my own eyes, and I won't believe anything he has to say anyway—not after this. I just need to get out of here, and fast.

I move to shove past him when his fingers curl around my bicep. He tightens his grip when I try to pull away and reaches for my other arm with his free hand. When he forces me to turn and look at him, the anger in his features shocks me. I don't think I've ever seen him mad like this.

"How's any of this *my* fault?" he asks through gritted teeth. The question confuses me so much that I just stare at him, unable to answer. How is it *not* his fault? "It's not like you're ever really around anymore. And even when you are, you always have some sort of excuse—"

"Are you insane?" I scream, cutting him off. "I've been working *two jobs* because we're supposed to be saving to buy a house! It was your fucking idea in the first place! I was under the impression that we were *both* working two jobs. Apparently, that was just a cover so you could go around behind my back, fucking anyone and everyone y—"

My words are cut off when he slaps me across the face, head whipping to the side, jaw dropping. Bringing my hand to my cheek, I turn to look at him. I don't know what I was expecting, but it definitely wasn't the smug, satisfied look on his face. Almost like this was something he'd been wanting to do for a while.

Tugging my arm out of his grasp, I turn to leave. He doesn't try to stop me this time, doesn't even bother to say anything else.

As I open the front door, a thought occurs to me and I yell into the apartment, "And tell your little friend to stop *following* me!"

Slamming the door before he has a chance to respond, I then hurry to my car.

I sit in the driver's seat of my car, looking in the mirror at the welt on my face. I already know it's going to bruise. Now I have to think about how I'm going to explain it to people at work. And I must've bitten my tongue when he slapped me because I can taste the metallic flavour of blood in my mouth.

I try to even out my breathing as I think about where to go. Maybe my mother's house? But seeing as she's the most judgemental person I've ever met, I'm going to avoid that for as long as I possibly can. Besides, she never liked Jack, always trying to warn me that he was going to break my heart and that he wasn't right for me. I'm not ready to listen to the, "I told you so."

Once, I would've just gone to my best friend Sydney's house, but after what she did, I'll probably never speak to her again. Racking my brain, trying to think of anywhere else I can go, I come up with nothing. I sit in the parking lot for far longer than I should—long enough for Jack to have come after me if he'd wanted to—when I finally have an idea.

Backing out of my parking spot, I head towards the closest shopping centre. It's summertime, and I have some savings, so I figure I can just buy a tent and an air mattress and find a campground nearby until I can find somewhere better to stay. It's not the greatest plan, but it beats sleeping in my car.

Want More?

If you're interested in keeping up with my work in progress, or any of my future books, you can use the QR code below to find my social media links!

Made in the USA
Monee, IL
07 July 2026

56550091R00069